For Sayuri

CHAPTERS

FOREWORD:
The Top-Secret Truth About Captain Underpants   7

1. George and Harold   15
2. Let's Get Serious, Folks!   23
3. Tippy Returns *Again*!   26
4. Fixing the Future   38
5. Tiny Tippy's Tremendous Task   49
6. 65 Million Years Ago   56
7. Two Tiny Traitors   62
8. Mission Improbable   66
9. Meanwhile, Seven Pages Ago . . .   72
10. What *Really* Killed the Dinosaurs   81
11. 206,784 Years Ago   87
12. Calling All Cavepeople   94
13. The World's Oldest Comic
    (Starring Ook and Gluk)   101
14. Clash of the Cavepeople   125

15. The Incredibly Graphic Violence Chapter, Part 1 (in Flip-O-Rama™)   135

16. What *Really* Caused the Ice Age   150

17. Have an Ice Day!   158

18. Something Much Less Far-Fetched   162

19. The Vow   167

20. Thirty Years from Now   171

21. George and Harold's Worst Nightmare   178

22. The Incredibly Graphic Violence Chapter, Part 2 (in Flip-O-Rama™)   185

23. How the Universe *Really* Began   198

24. To Make a Long Story Short   206

25. The Big *Ka-Bloosh!* Theory   208

26. What Have We Learned Today?   210

27. Meanwhile, Thirty Years from Now . . .   213

28. The Final Chapter of the Very Last Captain Underpants Epic Novel   217

THE Top SECRET TRUTH About CAPTAIN UNDERPANTS

It was funny at first...

Ha Ha Ha Ha Ha

Tra La Laaaa!

But then Mr. Krupp jumped out the window.

WAit!!!

mr. Krupp really thought he was captain underpants. He got in Lots of tRuBBeL!!!

COme BACK, Bub!

no way!

I'm a Hero!

One time a Big monster atacked the School.

rar!

it tried to eat up Mr. Krupp.

George Found Some super power Juice in a U.F.O.

S.P.J.

gLUB gLUB

Drink up, Bub!

Then mr. Krupp got super powers.

POW

how He can even FLy and stuff.

Tra-La Laaaaa!

The worst part is, whenever mr. Krupp hears somebuddy snap their fingers...

snap!

..He turns into captain Underpants.

...and whenever Captain Underpants gets water on his head...

He turns back into MR. KRUPP.

Blah Blah Blah

SO Any-WA-YS...

In our Last advencher, there was a evil guy named Tippy Tinkletrousers.

Thats me!

He bilt a Big ROBO-suit.

Then he climed inside.

Im going to D-estroy Captain Underpants!!!

Oh yeah?

They got in a big ~~Fight~~ Fight.

Behold my ice Ray!

missed me!

zong

zap

Tippy aksidentilly frozed his feet to the ground.

OH no my feet are frozed!

Ha Ha!

CLANK

Rats! you Broke my Robot

But Tippys Robot Pants was also a Time mashine!

I'm going To exscape by going back in Time!!!

Oh No!

NOW the future is changed. Everything is diffrent!!!

sinse Mr. krupp got fired 5 years ago...

Why me?

..He never got Hipnitized by George and Harold.

?

sinse Mr. krupp dident get Hipnitized...

Boo Hoo!

..He never turned into captain Underpants.

sinse captain Underpants dosent exist...

who's That?

He wasnt there to save the world !!!!!

Who will save us?

Beats me.

TIPPY REALIZED his misteak when he came back to the present.

OH NO! the world got destroyed!

ALL Because I scared those Bullys!

TIPPY Vowed To Make things RiGht.

I WILL FiX This Mess!

But Then...

UH OH!

STOMP

WHO WILL SAVE US NOW?

CHAPTER 1
GEORGE AND HAROLD

This is George Beard and Harold Hutchins.
George is the giant zombie nerd on the left
with the tie and the flat-top. Harold is the
giant zombie nerd on the right with the
T-shirt and the bad haircut.

Remember that now.

If you read our last adventure, you may recall the final terrifying scene where Tippy Tinkletrousers ended up cowering beneath the gigantic foot of Zombie Nerd Harold. You were probably horrified when the super-sized shoe slammed down to the ground, leaving behind a squishy, red stain. You may even have commented on the surprising inappropriateness of such a murderous and bloody scene appearing in a children's book. It's fun to feel offended, isn't it?

Unfortunately, I'm sorry to have to tell you that there was no murder at the end of the last book. There wasn't even any blood. What happened at the end of our last story is something called *misdirection*. It's what happens when you are led to believe that something is true, but in reality it's not true at all. Misdirection happens a lot in real life — especially in politics, history, education, medicine, marketing, science, religion, and the Oprah Winfrey Network.

With all of that misdirection out there, life can get a little confusing. But don't worry, this epic novel contains no misdirection whatsoever. This legendary tome will explain everything, from our recent narrative complexities to the vast mysteries of our universe. By the time you get to page 210, you'll know it all. You'll be a genius! You'll be smarter than the most brilliant scientist who ever walked the Earth.

So let's get started, shall we?

If you've ever been to the zoo, you might have noticed that really big creatures move kind of slowly. Take elephants for example. They don't move very fast—even when they're in a hurry. Sure, they might cover a lot of ground, but that's only because they're so big. If you were to shrink an elephant down to the size of a house cat, you'd be SHOCKED at how long it takes for them to get from one place to another. They're so darned slow that it wouldn't be long before somebody changed the story of "The Tortoise and the Hare" into the more appropriate "The Miniature Elephant and the Hare."

It's the same thing with lunchroom zombie nerds. Sure, they're big and scary and stuff, but they move reeeeeeeeeeeally slowly. So if a zombie nerd ever lifts his foot over you with the intent of stomping you into a puddle, don't worry. You actually have a few minutes before you're in any real danger.

Tippy found this out the hard way. When Zombie Nerd Harold lifted his foot above Tippy's head, Tippy screamed in horror. Then Tippy screamed again . . . and again. Then he checked his watch and screamed some more.

Finally, Tippy's voice got a little scratchy from all that screaming, so he got up and walked over to one of the few remaining stores on the planet to buy some cherry throat lozenges.

While he was there, he purchased a new suit and bow tie, read part of a magazine, and got a foot massage. On his way out of the store, Tippy noticed an extra-large novelty catsup pack that was on sale, so he bought it and dragged it back to the scene of the crime. Zombie Nerd Harold's shoe was still coming down slowly as Tippy placed the extra-large novelty catsup pack under it and walked away.

Tippy climbed back into his Robo-Pants just
as Zombie Nerd Harold's shoe hit the pavement
and crushed the giant novelty catsup pack.
A bright red stain squished out from beneath
the zombified shoe as Tippy's Robo-Pants
disappeared in a crackling glow of light. You
see, Tippy had mistakenly caused some trouble
the last time he had gone back in time, so he
had to go back *again* to undo the damage he
had done.

But before I can tell you that story, I have
to give you *this* warning . . .

CHAPTER 2
LET'S GET SERIOUS, FOLKS!

Did you ever notice how grown-ups hate it when kids are having fun? Seriously, when was the last time you were doing something fun and some adult came over and made you stop? If you're like most kids, you're probably reading this very book because some adult wanted you to quit playing video games or watching TV.

If you don't believe me, try this experiment: Grab a few of your friends, go into the corner of a room, and start goofing around. Make some noise! Start laughing and cheering and maybe shout out a "Woo-hoo!" or two. It's been scientifically proven that 89.4 percent of all grown-ups will drop whatever they're doing and rush over to put a stop to whatever "nonsense" you're up to.

You have to wonder, why are most grown-ups like this? Weren't they ever kids themselves? Didn't *they* enjoy laughing and cheering and goofing around when they were young? If so, when did they stop? And why?

Now, I certainly can't speak for *all* adults, but I'm going to anyway.

I think it's a lot easier for adults to stomp out someone else's fun than it is for them to reflect on their own lives and figure out where it all went so miserably wrong. It's just too depressing for grown-ups to ponder all the decades of compromises, failures, laziness, fear, and regrettable choices that slowly transformed them from running, jumping, laughing, fun-loving kids into grumpy,

complaining, calorie-counting, easily offended, peace-and-quiet-demanding grouches.

In other words, it's harder to look within yourself than it is to shout, "HEY, YOU KIDS, *CUT THAT OUT!*"

Keeping this in mind, you might not want to smile or laugh while reading this book. And when you get to the Flip-O-Rama parts, I suggest you flip with a bored, disinterested look on your face or some adult will probably take this book away from you and make you read *Sarah, Plain and Tall* instead.

Don't say I didn't warn you.

CHAPTER 3
TIPPY RETURNS *AGAIN!*

Tippy Tinkletrousers was in big trouble. He had zapped himself back in time five years and accidentally frightened four bullies. This thoughtless mistake set in motion a series of events that ultimately got Mr. Krupp fired. And since there was no Mr. Krupp, there was no Captain Underpants. And since there was no Captain Underpants, there was nobody to save the world from the terrible devastation caused by the villains from our first three epic novels.

Tippy decided there was only one thing to do: go back in time and *stop* himself from scaring those bullies. But in order to do this, he would have to go back in time *before* the last time he had gone back in time.

So Tippy set his Tinkle-Time Travelometer for ten minutes BEFORE the last time he had arrived in the past, and pressed the "Away We Go!" button.

After several seconds of made-for-television-styled special effects, Tippy found himself transported to the awful night of the terrifying thunderstorm. Everything looked very familiar. He knew at any moment, the four bullies would come running from the school and tear across the football field. Then they would come face-to-face with him (well, a slightly *younger* version of him), and only *he* could stop it all from happening.

Tippy hid behind the side of the school and waited as the wind howled ferociously. Suddenly, a brilliant flash of lightning struck a nearby power line. The electricity in the school went out, and all of the windows became dark.

Tippy listened closely and heard the sounds of squealing and slapping and shuffling. It sounded as if a terrible struggle was taking place inside the school. Then suddenly, the back door of the school crashed open, and the four petrified bullies shoved their way outside. Quickly, they darted toward the football field. This was Tippy's big chance.

He aimed his Freezy-Beam 4000 at the running delinquents and zapped them all with a mini-mountain of molecularly modified ice.

The four bullies were frozen in place.
Tippy scanned the boys with his life-systems
monitor and found them to be perfectly
preserved. The carbonite-and-tibanna-gas-
infused ice had been programmed to remain
solid for fifteen minutes—just long enough
for Tippy to do his thing.

Quickly, Tippy turned toward the football
field, where a ball of blue lightning was
growing bigger and bigger. Suddenly, it
exploded in a blinding flash.

And there, where the ball of lightning had been, was a giant pair of robotic pants.

"Boy, that was a close one," said a voice from inside the depths of the newly arrived Robo-Pants. "Captain Underpants is a lot stronger than I thought!"

The zipper of the newly arrived robotic trousers opened, and a tiny man peeked out to marvel at the world of five years ago.

But to his surprise, he saw an identical
copy of himself staring straight at him and
tapping *his* gigantic robotic foot impatiently.

"Who are *you*?" asked the newly arrived
Tippy.

"I'm *YOU*!" shouted Future Tippy. "You
from the future!"

"What's going on?" asked Tippy.

31

"I'm here to stop you from scaring those
kids over there!" said Future Tippy, pointing
at the frozen bullies.

"Why?" said Tippy. "What's so important
about those kids?"

"I have no idea," said Future Tippy. "All
I know is, I scared those kids when I came
back here last time, and apparently it caused
a chain reaction that resulted in the total
destruction of the Earth, more or less!"

"I see," said Tippy. "So what do we do now?"

Future Tippy looked at his watch. "Those kids are going to thaw out in eight minutes and eleven seconds," he said. "We've got to be gone by then!" So he reached into the cockpit of his Robo-Pants and grabbed one of his very first inventions, the Shrinky-Pig 2000. Tippy aimed it at the younger version of himself and pressed the button.

BLLLLLLZZZZRRRRK!

A powerful beam of energy blasted the newly arrived Tippy Tinkletrousers (and his gigantic pair of Robo-Pants) and shrunk them down to the size of a baseball.

Big Tippy reached down and picked up the tiny version of himself.

"What did you do that for?" shouted Tiny Tippy.

"I can't very well have TWO of us running around," said Big Tippy. "I've gotta keep an eye on you!" Big Tippy tucked Tiny Tippy into his jacket pocket and checked his watch again.

"Four minutes and sixteen seconds!" he muttered to himself. He looked over at the four bullies encased in the now-cracking ice mound. Big Tippy turned to his Tinkle-Time Travelometer and programmed it for a date in the future. Time was running out. The ice around the bullies was disintegrating fast, so Tippy sneaked away to the center of town, pressed his "Away We Go!" button, and disappeared into a ball of blue lightning.

Two seconds later, the ice mountain that had encased and preserved the bullies disintegrated completely. Without skipping a beat, the four frightened friends continued their mad dash away from the school.

   As they ran across the football field toward
their homes, something about Kipper and
his friends changed forever. They would
never again be the same despicable bullies
they once were.

CHAPTER 4
FIXING THE FUTURE

Big Tippy had set his Tinkle-Time Travelometer for a sunny afternoon in October, four years in the future. He arrived, as usual, in a giant ball of blue lightning that grew bigger and bigger, until it exploded in a blinding flash.

"What's going on out there?" cried Tiny Tippy. "I can't see a thing!"

"*SSSHHHH!!!*" shushed Big Tippy, as he shoved Tiny Tippy down into the deep, darkened depths of his jacket pocket. Big Tippy listened carefully. He heard the voice of a child muttering, "This can't be good."

Tippy unzipped the zipper of his Robo-Pants and peeked out. To his delight, the world looked like it usually did. No destruction, no giant zombie nerds, no moon rocks. Everything seemed pretty normal.

"Hey! It's Professor Poopypants!" shouted a small boy, whom Tippy recognized immediately.

Suddenly, two cops standing nearby started to laugh, which angered Tippy.

"Stop LAUGHING!" shouted Tippy. "My name is no longer Professor Poopypants. I changed it to Tippy Tinkletrousers!"

The two cops laughed even harder.

"And I've got a *special surprise* for anybody who thinks my NEW name is funny!" said the furious professor.

Tippy pressed the button on his Freezy-Beam 4000, causing it to rise from the depths of his Robo-Pants. He set the freeze ray for twenty minutes and zapped the cops, transforming them into frozen statues.

"My Freezy-Beam 4000 will take care of anybody who stands in my way!" said Tippy. "And now," he said with a wicked smile, "it's time for my *revenge*!"

"OH, NO!" screamed George.

"HERE WE GO AGAIN!" screamed Harold.

Tippy chased George and Harold and their two pets, Sulu and Crackers, through town, zapping his Freezy-Beam 4000 at them and laughing maniacally. The chase lasted all afternoon and into the night. The four friends hid behind buildings, inside trash bins, under bridges, and even down in the sewer. But it didn't matter where they sought refuge because Tippy Tinkletrousers always found them.

By the morning of the next day, our heroes had found a hiding place behind some bushes near the park.

"What are we going to do?" whispered George. "There's nowhere else to hide!"

"I don't know," whispered Harold.

George and Harold looked at their two pets, shivering with them in the morning mist.

"*We're* not going to make it," whispered George. "But there's no reason that Sulu and Crackers should have to suffer."

Harold's eyes began to water. "You're right," he whispered.

George and Harold petted their two friends sadly as they devised a plan to return to the dinosaur age. "We could use the Purple Potty to take Crackers back home where we found him," said George.

"Yeah," said Harold. "And Sulu could stay there with him. They'll both be safe there!"

As soon as it was clear, the four friends sneaked away from the bushes and headed for Jerome Horwitz Elementary School, carefully avoiding major streets and intersections. It was almost noon by the time George and Harold and their two pets reached the school. Cautiously, they sneaked through the front door and dashed up the stairs to the library.

"HEY, BUBS!" shouted Mr. Krupp angrily. "WHERE HAVE YOU KIDS BEEN?"

George and Harold looked down and saw Mr. Krupp carrying a large cardboard box. *"WELL?"* Mr. Krupp shouted. "GET DOWN HERE AND EXPLAIN YOURSELVES!"

George and Harold looked at their two pets and continued running up the stairs.

Mr. Krupp was FURIOUS. His day hadn't started out very well. For some strange reason, all the red curtains in his office had been disappearing, and he wasn't happy about it. So Mr. Krupp had driven angrily to the store, bought a replacement box of curtains, started a big fight with the cashier, got a flat tire on the way home, and now his *truant* students were bringing *animals* into the school, *ignoring* his commands, and *running* up the stairs.

"YOU KIDS GET BACK HERE!" shouted Mr. Krupp, as he chased after the four frightened friends. George and Harold and Crackers and Sulu raced to the top of the stairs, dashed into the library, and locked the door behind them.

There they beheld their old, troublesome nemesis, the Purple Potty. It was a homemade time machine that had a few quirks, to say the least, and our heroes approached it cautiously.

"Do you still remember how to use this thing?" asked Harold.

"Of course," said George. "We just used it yesterday morning! All I have to do is set the controller for sixty-five million years ago, then pull down on the chain. Easy, squeezy, mac-n-cheezy!"

Suddenly, Mr. Krupp reached the library door and struggled with the locked doorknob. The boys heard a shuffling sound, followed by the jingling of keys.

"Let's boogie!" cried George.

The four friends climbed into the Purple
Potty, and George closed the door. At that
very moment, Mr. Krupp came crashing
through the library door with his box of red
curtains. He ran to the Purple Potty and
banged on the door. "I KNOW YOU'RE IN
THERE," he screamed. "YOU CAN'T HIDE
FROM ME FOREVER!"

"Hurry!" cried Harold, as George fiddled
with the controller. "We've got to get out of
here!"

"I'm working as fast as I can!" cried George.

Suddenly, a gigantic dark shadow filled
the library. Mr. Krupp turned to see a huge,
robotic pair of trousers at the window. The
zipper unzipped, and Tippy Tinkletrousers
peeked through the cavernous opening.
"I'VE GOT YOU NOW!" he shouted. "HAW!
HAW! HAW!"

Tippy reached for the button on his
Freezy-Beam 4000 as Mr. Krupp cowered
in terror.

At that very moment, George finished
setting the controller for sixty-five million
years ago. Then he pulled down on the chain.

All at once, there was a brilliant flash of
green light, and the Purple Potty (along with
Mr. Krupp and his cardboard box) disappeared
into a whirlwind of electrified ozone.

CHAPTER 5
TINY TIPPY'S
TREMENDOUS TASK

"RATS!" screamed Tippy, as he watched the Purple Potty disappear. "Those kids have a time machine, and I don't know where they went!"

"What's going on?" cried Tiny Tippy from the depths of Big Tippy's pocket. "I can't see a thing!"

"Those kids took off in a time machine," Big Tippy barked at the miniature version of himself. "And they took Captain Underpants with them!"

"Where did they go?" asked Tiny Tippy.

"How should I know?" Big Tippy yelled.

"Hey! I've got an idea," said Tiny Tippy. "Why don't *I* go back in time and find out?"

"Good idea, me!" said Big Tippy. He reached down and placed Tiny Tippy in the library. "You go back in time ten minutes and listen to everything they say. Then when I show up, tell me where they went!"

"You got it!" said Tiny Tippy. He set his Tinkle-Time Travelometer for "Ten Minutes Ago," and in a blue-crackling instant, he was gone.

Tiny Tippy arrived in the same spot he had left, only it was now ten minutes earlier. He heard some people running up the stairs, so he decided to hide behind a trash can. Suddenly, George, Harold, and their two pets dashed into the room and locked the door behind them.

Tiny Tippy watched as the boys tiptoed toward the tall, time-traveling toilet.

"Do you still remember how to use this thing?" asked Harold.

"Of course," said George. "We just used it yesterday morning! All I have to do is set the controller for sixty-five million years ago, then pull down on the chain. Easy, squeezy, mac-n-cheezy!"

"A-HA!" muttered Tiny Tippy. "They're going back in time to the Mesozoic era!"

Tiny Tippy watched as the four friends climbed into the time machine and closed the door. He saw Mr. Krupp crash through the library door and bang on the lavender lavatory. Then he saw himself (the big version of himself, that is) appear at the window.

"I'VE GOT YOU NOW!" shouted Big Tippy. "HAW! HAW! HAW!"

Suddenly, there was a brilliant flash of green light, and the Purple Potty (along with Mr. Krupp and his cardboard box) disappeared into a whirlwind of electrified ozone.

"RATS!" screamed Tippy, as he watched the Purple Potty disappear. "Those kids have a time machine, and I don't know where they went!"

"I do," said Tiny Tippy, as he stepped out from behind the garbage can.

"Who are you?" asked Big Tippy.

"I'm Tiny Tippy!" said Tiny Tippy.

"That's impossible," said Big Tippy. "Tiny Tippy is right here!" He reached into his pocket and pulled out the miniature version of himself, who had been complaining because he couldn't see a thing.

"I'm ten minutes older than that guy," said Tiny Tippy. "You sent me back in time so I could find out where those kids went to."

"Oh! I get it," said Big Tippy. "Good idea, me! So where'd they go?"

"They went backward in time to sixty-five million years ago!" said Tiny Tippy.

"A-HA!" said Big Tippy and Slightly Younger Tiny Tippy to themselves, simultaneously. "They're going back in time to the Mesozoic era!"

Big Tippy picked up Tiny Tippy and shoved him into his pocket next to Slightly Younger Tiny Tippy. "Let's all go back to the dinosaur age, shall we? If we time it right, we can get there just before that Purple Potty arrives!"

CHAPTER 6
65 MILLION YEARS AGO

The primitive midday sky lit up with several
blinding flashes as the Purple Potty suddenly
appeared in the top of an ancient tree. George
and Harold had successfully brought Crackers
back to where they had found him. But when
they opened the door of the Purple Potty, they
discovered they'd also brought a stowaway.

"WHAT THE HECK IS GOING ON HERE?"
cried Mr. Krupp, as he hung from a branch
high up in the treetop.

"Oh, NO!" cried George. "Mr. Krupp must
have been standing too close to the Purple
Potty when we zapped backward in time. He
got zapped back with us!"

Harold reached out his hand to grab hold of
Mr. Krupp. "How could things get any worse?"
he asked.

Suddenly, the tree started to shake. *BOOM!*
BOOM! BOOM! went the tree.

George and Harold looked down and saw
Tippy's gigantic Robo-Pants kicking the side
of the tree.

"What's *HE* doing here?" cried Harold.

"I don't know," said George, "but I think
we're about to fall!"

The horrible kicking continued and the tree shook wildly. Finally, the Purple Potty slid sideways and toppled over. "We're DOOMED!" screamed Harold, as they all fell. The Purple Potty cracked and split apart as it tumbled down the side of the tree. Mr. Krupp fell, too, smacking against every branch on the way down. Suddenly, the Purple Potty hit the ground with a terrible crash and broke apart into a thousand pieces.

Mr. Krupp hit the ground, too, but was surprised to find out that he wasn't hurt a bit.

Big Tippy kicked through the wreckage of the Purple Potty but could not find any trace of George or Harold or their pets. "Where did they go?" he asked.

"Look! Up there!" cried the two Tiny Tippys, who were peeking out of Big Tippy's pocket.

Crackers had grabbed George and Harold and Sulu at the last second. "Good boy, Crackers!" cried George. "You saved us!"

"NOT FOR LONG!" screamed Big Tippy, as he peered peevishly from a porthole on top of his Robo-Pants.

George and Harold looked down at Mr. Krupp, who was still trying to figure out how he'd fallen sixty feet and not gotten hurt. The two boys snapped their fingers.

Suddenly, a welcome smile spread across Mr. Krupp's face. Immediately, he pulled off his shoes and socks. Then he unclipped his tie and ripped off his shirt. He grabbed a red curtain from the cardboard box beside him and tied it around his neck as he wiggled out of his pants.

Captain Underpants was BACK! And Tippy Tinkletrousers and his two tiny twins were in for the fight of their lives!

CHAPTER 7
TWO TINY TRAITORS

George and Harold ran through the thick jungle foliage, with Crackers and Sulu flying above them.

Captain Underpants decided to tag along, too, just for fun.

Big Tippy jumped onto the back of a nearby Tyrannosaurus rex and chased after them.

"YOU CAN'T RUN FOREVER!" shouted Big Tippy. "When I catch you guys, I'm gonna tear you apart!"

"Can we help?" asked the two Tiny Tippys, who were tucked away in Big Tippy's jacket pocket.

"NO!" yelled Big Tippy sternly. "You two keep quiet while I take care of business. This is a job for a *MAN*, not two little twerps like you!"

As the chase continued, the two Tiny Tippys grumbled to themselves. "Boy, I'm getting tired of that giant jerk bossing us around!" said Tiny Tippy.

"Me, too!" said Slightly Younger Tiny Tippy. "He thinks he's such a big shot just because he's *HUGE*!"

"I sure wish I still had my Goosy-Grow 4000," said Tiny Tippy. "Then I could make myself big again!"

"I was just thinking the same thing!" said Slightly Younger Tiny Tippy. "But unfortunately, we stored the Goosy-Grow 4000 in the top half of our Robo-Suit, and Captain Underpants destroyed it back in chapter 8 of our last epic novel!"

"Hey," cried Tiny Tippy, "why don't we go back—er, I mean forward in time to chapter 8 of our last epic novel? We could grab that Goosy-Grow 4000 and make ourselves *GIGANTIC*!"

"I like the way you think, me!" said Slightly Younger Tiny Tippy.

So while Big Tippy chased everybody through the treacherous jungles of the Cretaceous period, the two Tiny Tippys set their Tinkle-Time Travelometers for the night of the big battle from chapter 8 of our last epic novel. Big Tippy was so engrossed in his pursuit of our heroes, he didn't even notice the teensy-weensy blue sparks of flashing light emanating from his pocket as his two devious doppelgängers disappeared in a whiff of primeval troposphere.

CHAPTER 8
MISSION IMPROBABLE

Instantly, the two tiny Tippys zapped forward in time, only to find themselves knee-deep in something creamy, coconutty, and marshmallowy.

"Honey?" said a mother who was setting her dinner table. "Two little pairs of pants are walking around in our ambrosia salad!"

"Oh, *really*?" said her son. "And *I'm* the one seeing a therapist!"

Tiny Tippy and Slightly Younger Tiny Tippy
crawled out of the serving bowl and shook off
the pineapple chunks and mandarin orange
slices that had stuck to their legs. Then they
jumped to the floor and slipped through the
mail slot in the front door.

Outside, they could hear the crashing
sounds of the terrifying battle between Captain
Underpants and Big Tippy. The two tiny Tippys
ran toward the noises until they arrived at the
school's football field. Captain Underpants had
just started pulling on Tippy's Robo-Arms.

One by one, the rivets in the Robo-Suit's thick, steel belt began to pop. Captain Underpants yanked and tugged and pulled, and finally the Robo-Suit tore in half with a terrible *CLANK*!

Tiny Tippy and Slightly Younger Tiny Tippy ran over to the place where Captain Underpants had dropped the upper portion of the Robo-Suit. Quickly, they searched through the twisted metal until they found what they were looking for: the Goosy-Grow 4000.

Outside, they could hear the crackling sounds of Big Tippy zapping himself backward in time. A blinding flash lit up the nighttime sky as the two Tippys dragged the Goosy-Grow 4000 from the wreckage and carried it away with them through the parking lot.

Soon, they came to a darkened street
behind some old warehouses. "OK," said Tiny
Tippy. "You zap me, then I'll zap you!"

"Hey!" said Slightly Younger Tiny Tippy.
"How come *you* get to go first?"

"Because I'm slightly older than you," said
Tiny Tippy. "And slightly more mature!"

"Alright, alright," said Slightly Younger
Tiny Tippy, who could not argue with the fact
that Tiny Tippy was indeed ten minutes more
mature than himself. "Let's just do this thing
and get it over with!"

He aimed the Goosy-Grow 4000 at Tiny
Tippy and jumped up on the button.

And before you could even say
"GGGGLLUUZZZZZZZRRRRRT!" a beam of
energy zapped Tiny Tippy, causing him to grow
thirty feet tall.

"Zap me again!" said Tiny Tippy.

"Alright," said Slightly Younger Tiny Tippy. "But then you'll zap me, right?"

"Sure! Sure!" said Tiny Tippy. "I promise!"

GGGGLLUUZZZZZZZZRRRRRT! went another bright beam of energy. This time Tiny Tippy grew to be sixty feet tall. "HAW! HAW! HAW!" he laughed. "BEHOLD! I HAVE BEEN REBORN AS *SUPA MEGA TIPPY*!"

"My turn! My turn!" cried Slightly Younger Tiny Tippy.

Supa Mega Tippy reached down and grabbed the Goosy-Grow 4000. He tucked it into the cup holder on his electrical panel and waved good-bye to Slightly Younger Tiny Tippy.

"HEY!" cried Slightly Younger Tiny Tippy. "What about ME?"

"Sorry," said Supa Mega Tippy. "But this is a job for a *MAN*, not a little twerp like you!!!"

CHAPTER 9
MEANWHILE,
SEVEN PAGES AGO . . .

Sixty-five million years earlier, Big Tippy
had chased our heroes to the jagged edge of
a cliff overlooking a lake. Crackers grabbed
George and Harold by their shirt collars, and
they all sailed safely over the edge of the cliff
to join Captain Underpants in the clouds.

Big Tippy's Tyrannosaurus rex screeched to a halt at the cliff's edge and roared ferociously at the five floating friends.

"We won!" Captain Underpants laughed at Tippy. "Now it's our turn to chase you!"

"This isn't a *game*," yelled Big Tippy. "This is *serious*!" He leaped off of the neck of the T. rex and grabbed Captain Underpants with his patented, robotic Extendo-Flex Mechani-Gripper. Together they fell a thousand feet into the lake below.

When they emerged from the depths of the lake, something had changed. Tippy was still just as mean and ornery as ever, but Captain Underpants looked different.

"WHAT THE HECK IS GOING ON HERE?" yelled the angry-looking hero.

"Oh, NO!" cried George. "Captain Underpants got water on his head! He changed back into Mr. Krupp!"

"Quick, Crackers," called Harold. "Fly us down there as fast as you can!" Crackers glided down toward the tempestuous struggle below, and the boys snapped their fingers with all their might.

But it did no good. Mr. Krupp's head was still soaking wet, so he could not change back into Captain Underpants.

"Well look what *I* just figured out!" cried Big Tippy. "Captain Underpants turns back into a crabby old elementary school principal whenever he gets wet!"

"You leave him alone!" yelled George, still snapping his fingers in vain.

"Yeah!" cried Harold. "It's not a fair fight anymore!"

"Wow!" laughed Big Tippy incredulously. "He's gotta be the world's *EASIEST* superhero to defeat! I could've destroyed him with a *SQUIRT GUN*!!!"

Suddenly, a blinding flash lit up the world around them. Then came the footsteps. Terrible, deafening, tumultuous footsteps that shook the Earth with each thundering stomp. Finally, a massive shadow spread across the lake. Big Tippy looked up.

It was Supa Mega Tippy.

"Hey!" shouted Big Tippy. He quickly checked his jacket pocket and found it to be empty. "Where'd you come from? How'd you get so big? Where's the other one?"

"None of that is important now," said Supa Mega Tippy. "What's important *now* is who's in charge!"

"Hey, you'll never believe this!" said Big Tippy, ignoring his diabolical double. "I just figured out that if you get Captain Underpants wet, he loses his super powers!"

"His weakness is *WATER*?" said Supa Mega Tippy. "Wow. *Really?*"

"I know!" said Big Tippy. "I couldn't believe it myself! Hey! I'm gonna destroy him real quick. Then we can get out of here and go rule the world and stuff!"

"*You're* not going to destroy him," said Supa Mega Tippy. "I am!"

"Now hold on, bub," said Big Tippy. "*I* caught him, so *I'm* gonna destroy him!"

"Oh, yeah?" said Supa Mega Tippy, with a growl that made the surface of the lake tremble. "Well I'm bigger than you, so *I'm* gonna decide who destroys who!" He took a giant step toward Big Tippy and reached down with an Extendo-Flex Mechani-Gripper.

"Not so fast!" cried Big Tippy. He pressed a button on his control panel, causing the back of his Robo-Pants to lower. Suddenly, a gigantic metal arm emerged from the depths of Tippy's giant Robo-Rear, revealing a forty-ton thermonuclear bomb.

"You take one step closer and I'll blow us all to smithereens!" said Big Tippy.

"You're forgetting something!" yelled Supa Mega Tippy. "I have a bomb, too! And it's a LOT bigger than yours!" Supa Mega Tippy took a step closer as Big Tippy pressed the button.

Suddenly, a light on the side of the bomb began to flash red. A computerized voice emanating from the bomb's arming system began the countdown: **"This bomb will detonate in sixty seconds,"** said the voice.

"YOU—YOU PRESSED THE BUTTON?!!?" screamed Supa Mega Tippy incredulously. "I CAN'T BELIEVE YOU ACTUALLY *PRESSED THE BUTTON*!"

"I don't *care!*" cried Big Tippy. "I've been working on my revenge for years! I'm not going to let you rob me of this moment! I don't care if it kills me, too!"

"This bomb will detonate in forty-five seconds," said the bomb.

"We can't turn these bombs off, you know," said Supa Mega Tippy. "Once the countdown starts, it's *OVER!*"

"I *told you*, I don't care!" said Big Tippy. "I just want to be the one who FINALLY DESTROYS CAPTAIN UNDERPANTS!"

Supa Mega Tippy reached down with an uncoiling Extendo-Flex Mechani-Gripper and cut Mr. Krupp free. "HEY!" screamed Big Tippy. "What are you doing?"

"He's MINE!" said Supa Mega Tippy, as he drew back his foot.

"But what about me?" said Big Tippy. "What about my bomb?"

"Your bomb, your problem!" said Supa Mega Tippy, as he kicked Big Tippy with all his might.

CHAPTER 10
WHAT *REALLY* KILLED
THE DINOSAURS

"Nooooooo!" screamed Big Tippy, as he sailed into the clouds at an incredible speed.

"This bomb will detonate in thirty seconds," said the bomb.

Big Tippy flew across North America, soaring faster and faster through the stratosphere.

"This bomb will detonate in fifteen seconds," said the bomb.

Big Tippy began to lose altitude as he sailed toward the Gulf of Mexico.

"This bomb will detonate in five seconds," said the bomb.

"4 . . . 3 . . . 2 . . . 1 . . ."

Finally, Big Tippy landed just off the coast of the Yucatán Peninsula with a violently colossal splashdown (as seen below).

PLIP!

The massive explosion that followed blew a chunk in the Earth fifteen miles deep and more than sixty miles wide. Terrible earthquakes shook the entire planet as a gigantic tsunami sent a towering wall of seawater rolling across the continents.

"What's happening?" cried George.

"It's that dumb nuclear bomb!" shouted Supa Mega Tippy. "It just triggered the start of the Cenozoic era. I'm gonna become *extinct* if I don't get out of here!" Quickly, Supa Mega Tippy set his Tinkle-Time Travelometer for 64,793,216 years into the future and pressed the "Away We Go!" button.

Suddenly, gigantic bolts of lightning began shooting out of Supa Mega Tippy's Robo-Pants as a ball of blue light enveloped him.

"Quick, Crackers!" cried Harold, as thick volcanic ash began blocking out the sun. "Fly into the blue light! It's our only chance to escape!"

Crackers pointed his long reptilian neck toward the crackling orb, and the four friends sailed downward into the blinding blue lightning.

CHAPTER 11
206,784 YEARS AGO

A flash of white light filled the mid-afternoon haze of the Pleistocene epoch. The crystal-blue lake that had once been there was now gone. In its place were vast savanna plains stretching out to thick, forested hillsides and rocky caves. All was quiet, except for the sounds of insects and birds, and a faint rhythmic drumming far off in the forest.

"Where are we?" asked George.

"I think the better question would be, '*When* are we?'" said Harold.

Supa Mega Tippy was surprised to see George and Harold and Crackers and Sulu. "Well, well, well!" he said. "It looks like we have four stowaways!"

But what Supa Mega Tippy did not realize is that he had a *fifth* stowaway as well. It was Slightly Younger Tiny Tippy, who at that very moment was carefully crawling down a button on Supa Mega Tippy's shirt.

"That *Stupid* Mega Tippy thinks he can lie to *me* and get away with it," said Slightly Younger Tiny Tippy, as he jumped onto the control panel. "But I'll teach him a lesson he'll never forget!" Slightly Younger Tiny Tippy pried up an aluminum vent and slipped effortlessly into the wiry innards of the control panel. First, he reversed the polarity on the Emulsifying Sossilflange Inhibitor. Then he switched the blue and the green wires on the Reverse-Somgobulating Tracto-McFractionalizer. Finally, he snipped all the wires to the Freezy-Beam 4000's "Off" button.

"Haw! Haw! Haw!" laughed Slightly Younger Tiny Tippy. "The next time that big jerk uses his Freezy-Beam 4000, he's going to get a BIG SURPRISE!"

Meanwhile, the drama outside was getting serious. Supa Mega Tippy swatted at our heroes as they soared bravely through the Ionian sky. Crackers skillfully swooped and dived and loop-de-looped as the Extendo-Flex Mechani-Gripper whizzed after him.

But Supa Mega Tippy quickly became impatient and unleashed two *more* Extendo-Flex Mechani-Grippers. Poor Crackers could not outmaneuver them all, and the four friends were soon captured.

"I'VE GOT YOU NOW!" screamed Supa Mega Tippy.

"Hey, LOOK!" said George, pointing at the ground behind Supa Mega Tippy. "There's a bunch of cavepeople down there watching us!"

"I'm not falling for *that* trick!" said Supa Mega Tippy. "As soon as I turn around, you guys are going to try to escape!"

"NO, SERIOUSLY!" cried Harold. "We're not lying! Look behind you!"

Supa Mega Tippy glanced quickly and noticed that the boys were indeed telling the truth. Standing behind them at the edge of the forest were about a dozen very surprised-looking cavepeople staring up in dumbfounded bewilderment.

"You boys shouldn't be surprised to see cavepeople," said Supa Mega Tippy, as he studied the strange prehistoric people. "We're in the middle of the Pleistocene epoch. This is around the time that the first human families started to appear on Earth! I'll bet you dumb kids didn't know that, did you?"

Supa Mega Tippy turned to smile haughtily at George and Harold, but of course, they were gone. Sulu had bitten through three of the Extendo-Flex Mechani-Grippers, and the four friends had fluttered away.

"NOOOOOOOO!" screamed Supa Mega Tippy, as he stomped his gigantic feet in frustration. The startled cavepeople screamed and ran in terror back to their homes in the deep forest.

Supa Mega Tippy grabbed some strong vines
and tied Mr. Krupp to a boulder underneath
a waterfall.

"There!" he sneered. "This should keep you
moist and powerless until I get back!" Then he
stormed into the forest, searching for George
and Harold and their pets.

CHAPTER 12
CALLING ALL CAVEPEOPLE

"How are we ever going to get out of *THIS* mess?" asked Harold.

"I don't know," said George. "But we're going to need Tippy Tinkletrousers if we ever want to get back home!"

"Are you kidding?" said Harold. "We can't trust that guy! He can't even trust *himself*!"

"I know," said George. "But Tippy has a time machine, and we don't. So we're going to have to defeat him!"

"But we'd need an army to defeat that guy," said Harold.

"So let's go get an army," said George.

The four friends glided above the grassy plains as they followed the sounds of beating drums. Soon, they arrived at the forest.

The drumming was getting louder. Crackers swooped down and landed behind some bushes near the caves. Just beyond them was the cavepeople village.

George and Harold and Crackers and Sulu peeked over the thick bushes as they watched the cavepeople go about their daily routines. They seemed peaceful, so George decided to speak up.

"Hello!" said George. "We come in peace! We are friends!" The cavepeople looked confused and startled. They did not seem to understand.

"Maybe they don't speak English," said Harold.

"Ellohay!" said George (who only spoke one other language). "Eway omecay inway eacepay! Eway areway iendsfray!"

That didn't work either.

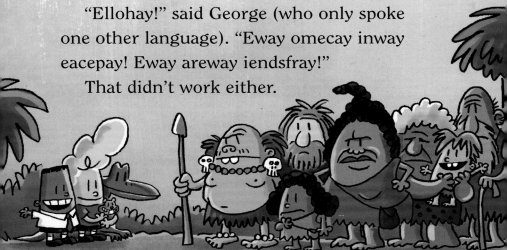

The cavepeople grunted and sniffed at George and Harold and their pets.

But they said nothing.

Suddenly, off in the distance, the sounds of gigantic footsteps came thundering through the deep forest. Tippy was coming, and he was getting closer and closer with each terrifying stomp.

"I KNOW YOU'RE IN THAT VILLAGE!" Tippy screamed. "But you can't hide from ME!!!"

Tippy crashed through the trees
and stomped into the village, kicking over
huts and smooshing everything in sight. The
terrified cavepeople grabbed their children
and ran for the safety of the caves behind their
village. George and Harold and Crackers and
Sulu ran into the caves also, and hid with the
cavepeople in the darkness as the destruction
outside continued.

After a while, some caveteenagers started a campfire. The flickering light illuminated the massive walls of the caves as the cavepeople whimpered and huddled together in horror.

"Wow!" said George. "Some army *they* turned out to be!"

"It's not their fault," said Harold. "They've never seen giant Robo-Pants before. They're just scared!"

"If we could only communicate with them," said George. "There's gotta be some way to reach them!"

Harold looked up at the giant, blank walls of the cave. "How about pictures?" he asked.

"Hey! Good idea," said George.

Harold walked over to the campfire and grabbed a charred, smoking stick from the burning cinders. Then he went to one side of the giant cave and started to create the world's first cave drawing.

At first, the cavepeople were astonished. They had never seen anybody draw before. They laughed and pointed and jumped up and down every time Harold drew something new.

But when Harold drew Tippy and his
Robo-Pants, the cavepeople became frightened.
They grunted nervously and lowered their
heads in fear and submission.

"Wow," said Harold. "How are we ever
gonna change their minds about Tippy?"

"I know," said George. "Let's make a
wordless comic! They'll understand that!"

"Good idea!" said Harold. "Let's do it!"

So George and Harold found a ladder and
began creating the world's very first comic.

The cavepeople watched with excitement
as George and Harold's tale unfolded. Soon,
their opinions about Tippy and his Robo-Pants
began to *evolve*.

CHAPTER 13
THE WORLD'S OLDEST COMIC
(STARRING OOK AND GLUK)

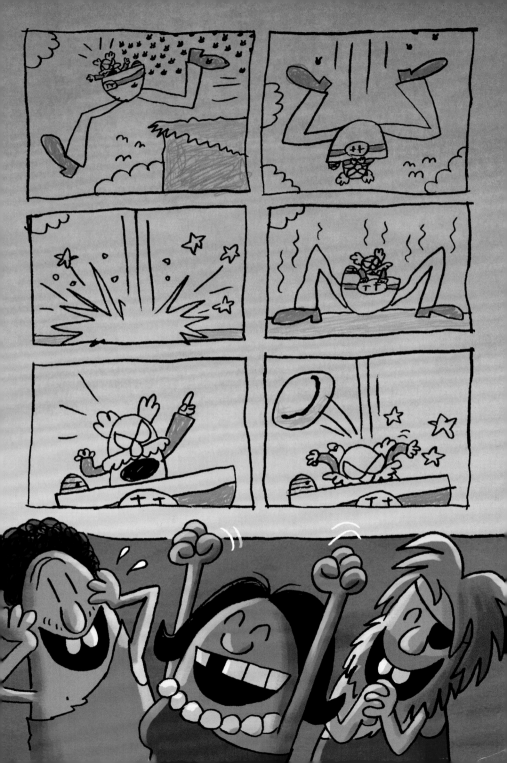

CHAPTER 14
CLASH OF THE CAVEPEOPLE

Once the cavepeople "read" George and Harold's cave comic, they stopped being afraid of Tippy and his Robo-Pants. Now they were inspired.

Quickly, they divided themselves into groups and began planning their counterattacks. George and Harold watched as the cavepeople grabbed their own charred sticks from the fire and began drawing out elaborate plans. Even though they could only speak in grunts and groans, they all understood comics, and they all knew what needed to be done.

Before long, everyone high-fived and sneaked out the back of the cave. The cavepeople ran up the hillside, tying vines between trees, placing banana peels all over the ground, and setting booby traps everywhere they could think of.

Once everyone was ready, George and Harold and Sulu hopped onto Crackers's back, and they flew around the cave to where Tippy was still busy destroying the village.

"Oh, TIPPY!" called George. "Where have you been? You're going to miss all the fun!"

Tippy turned quickly and chased after the four friends, who led him directly into the cavepeople's traps.

As Tippy ran, he glanced down and noticed
a vine tied tightly between two tree trunks.
Quickly, he screeched to a halt.

"Haw! Haw! Haw!" Tippy bellowed. "Did you
think I was going to fall for THAT lame trick?"
Tippy rolled his eyes in contempt as he jumped
over the vine . . .

. . . and landed on a bunch of banana peels.
"Yaaaaaa!" Tippy screamed, as he slipped
and crashed to the ground. Then Tippy started
sliding on the banana peels, down the steep
hill toward the cliff below.

"NOOOOOOO!" Tippy wailed as he slid faster and faster. Finally, Tippy flipped over the edge of the cliff and tumbled into the tar pit below with a mighty *Ker-Sploosh*!

Tippy was FURIOUS! He pulled himself up out of the sticky black tar and screamed, "Is that all you got?"

But the cavepeople had a few more surprises
in store for Tippy.

"YOU STUPID CAVEJERKS!" Tippy screamed, as he finally came to his senses. "IS THAT ALL YOU GOT???" But unfortunately for Tippy, there was still more to come.

"AAAAAAAAA!" screamed Tippy, as his tar-covered Robo-Butt caught on fire. Tippy ran shrieking toward a small pond as the flames spread everywhere.

Finally, the screaming robotic fireball plunged deep into the cooling waters of the pond with a gigantic splash. George, Harold, Crackers, Sulu, and the cavepeople gathered around the edge of the pond to see what had become of their evil nemesis. For a few minutes, everything was calm. Then the surface of the water began to tremble.

Suddenly, Tippy's bruised, battered, and burned Robo-Body rose from the bubbling depths of the pond.

"IS THAT ALL YOU GOT?!!?" Tippy demanded, as he lunged toward the cavepeople and chased after them.

But unfortunately for Tippy, they still had much more unpleasantness in store for him.

CHAPTER 15
THE INCREDIBLY GRAPHIC VIOLENCE CHAPTER, PART 1 (IN FLIP-O-RAMA™)

PILKEY® BRAND
O-RAMA

HERE'S HOW IT WORKS!

Step 1
First, place your *left* hand inside the dotted lines marked "LEFT HAND HERE." Hold the book open *flat*.

Step 2
Grasp the *right-hand* page with your right thumb and index finger (inside the dotted lines marked "RIGHT THUMB HERE").

Step 3
Now *quickly* flip the right-hand page back and forth until the picture appears to be *animated*.

(For extra fun, try adding your own sound-effects!)

FLIP-O-RAMA 1

(pages 139 and 141)

Remember, flip *only* page 139.
While you are flipping, be sure you
can see the picture on page 139
and the one on page 141.
If you flip quickly, the two
pictures will start to look like
<u>one</u> *animated* picture.

Don't forget to
add your own sound-effects!

LEFT HAND HERE

BOULDER BASH

RIGHT
THUMB
HERE

RIGHT
INDEX
FINGER
HERE

BOULDER BASH

FLIP-O-RAMA 2

(pages 143 and 145)

Remember, flip *only* page 143.
While you are flipping, be sure you
can see the picture on page 143
and the one on page 145.
If you flip quickly, the two
pictures will start to look like
<u>one</u> *animated* picture.

Don't forget to
add your own sound-effects!

LEFT HAND HERE

RHINO-BLASTY

RIGHT
THUMB
HERE

RIGHT
INDEX
FINGER
HERE

RHINO-BLASTY

FLIP-O-RAMA 3

(pages 147 and 149)

Remember, flip *only* page 147.
While you are flipping, be sure you
can see the picture on page 147
and the one on page 149.
If you flip quickly, the two
pictures will start to look like
<u>one</u> *animated* picture.

Don't forget to
add your own sound-effects!

LEFT HAND HERE

TIMBER TRAUMA

RIGHT
THUMB
HERE

RIGHT
INDEX
FINGER
HERE

148

TIMBER TRAUMA

CHAPTER 16
WHAT *REALLY* CAUSED
THE ICE AGE

"Is — is that — is that all you — you g-g-g — "
moaned Tippy, as he fell to his battered,
smoldering knees. Tippy's giant robotic pants
might have been a technological marvel, but
they were no match for caveperson cleverness.

Tippy was in trouble, but he still had one
last trick up his sleeve. He reached down to
his control panel and pressed the Freezy-Beam
4000's button. Suddenly, the battered top of the
Robo-Pants opened up, and the Freezy-Beam
4000 rose menacingly from the robotic innards.

Instantly, a massive burst of ice blasted at
the cavepeople. Fortunately, they all got out of
the way just in time, but the ice kept blasting
anyway.

"What's wrong with this thing?" said Tippy, as he pressed the Freezy-Beam 4000's "off" button repeatedly. The button was stuck, so Tippy pulled the Emergency Shut-Off Lever. That wouldn't budge either.

"It's almost as if someone has just tampered with my control panel!" said Tippy, unaware that tiptoeing across the floor at that very moment was someone who had just tampered with his control panel.

Slightly Younger Tiny Tippy, still angry that he had been betrayed by his treacherous twin, had rigged the Freezy-Beam 4000 so that it could never be turned off. Now the ice beam was going berserk.

Glaciers of synthetic ice, programmed to last for seventy thousand years, cascaded from Tippy's Freezy-Beam 4000, encasing the trees and securing his robotic feet to the frozen ground. Things were getting out of control. Tippy quickly crawled under his command center, desperately trying to figure out a way to turn off the spewing icebergs.

This was Slightly Younger Tiny Tippy's chance. He reached out with his Robo-Gloves and grabbed the Goosy-Grow 4000. Then, with a mighty leap, he jumped to the opening at the top of the robotic legs and hopped down to the frosty ground below.

The ice was spreading at a dangerous rate. Slightly Younger Tiny Tippy needed to act fast. With no time to spare, he grabbed a piece of bubble gum from his pocket, chewed it up, read the comic on the wrapper, then jammed the sticky bubble gum into the button of the Goosy-Grow 4000.

"Now," said Slightly Younger Tiny Tippy, "when I press this button down, it'll STICK!"— which is exactly what happened.

GGGGLLUUZZZZZZZZRRRRRT!

A continuous beam of growth energy burst forth from the goose-shaped contraption. Quickly, Slightly Younger Tiny Tippy jumped into the energy beam and grew to an impressive thirty feet tall.

"AWESOME!" cried Slightly Younger Tiny Tippy, as he jumped in front of the beam again and again, like a child leaping through a lawn sprinkler. Each time he hit the beam of energy, he grew another thirty feet.

"I'm HUGE!" cried Slightly Younger Tiny Tippy, who was now towering above the Earth at an impressive 120 feet. He reached down to pick up the Goosy-Grow 4000 with his Robo-Glove.

"Just a few more zaps and I'll be — whoops!" cried Slighty Younger Tiny Tippy, as the Goosy-Grow 4000 slipped out of his Robo-Glove and tumbled down onto the thick ice below him.

Unfortunately, the continuously zapping beam of energy was now pointed directly at the gigantic mountain of ice, which caused it to grow and expand and spread out even farther. Quickly, the ice began pushing its way east across the Ohio Valley and west into the part of the Earth that would one day be known as Indiana. Then it began shoving its way north into Michigan and Canada and beyond.

An accidental glacial period was developing rapidly, and Slightly Younger Tiny Tippy needed to get out of there fast if he wanted to avoid it.

CHAPTER 17
HAVE AN ICE DAY!

George and Harold grabbed their pets and ran as fast as they could to escape the rapidly spreading ice fields. Their cavebuddies were right behind them.

"Quick, Crackers," said George, "you've got to take Sulu and get out of here! It's your only hope!" But something was wrong with Crackers. The usually perky pterodactyl seemed to be getting sick.

"Maybe he's catching a cold," cried Harold. "He's not used to the freezing temperatures!"

Soon, they came upon the massive waterfall where Mr. Krupp was tied up.

The ice was already beginning to turn the flowing water into frozen slush.

"We've got to rescue Mr. Krupp!" said George.

"But there's no time!" said Harold. "We'll all get *frozed*!"

"We don't have a choice," said George. "We can't just leave him there!"

George and Harold ran toward Mr. Krupp and began pulling at the vines holding him in place. When the cavepeople saw what the boys were trying to do, they also stopped running and came forward to help.

But it was too late. The ice got closer and closer as everyone pulled desperately at the vines in the rapidly freezing water. The frigid, slushy water wrapped around Harold's shirt as thick ice encased George's body.

"Oh w-w-w-well," said Harold, as he shivered in the rapidly expanding permafrost, "at least w-w-we t-t-t-tried our b-b-b-best!"

"G-G-G-G-G-Good-bye," said George, as the
ice flowed up around his face and covered the
top of his head.

The end had finally come for George and
Harold. It was all over. The only hope they had
left was that maybe someday in the future,
an archaeologist would dig up their fossilized
bones and have a lot of explaining to do. But
even that hope seemed far-fetched at best.

CHAPTER 18
SOMETHING MUCH LESS FAR-FETCHED

CRASH!!!!

Suddenly, the ice around George and Harold and their cavebuddies shattered with a mighty karate chop.

"You didn't think I'd leave you behind, did you?" said Slightly Younger Tiny Tippy, as he scooped everyone up with one gigantic shovel of his Robo-Glove.

Everyone held on to one another for warmth as Slightly Younger Tiny Tippy trudged south across the frosty glaciers.

It was about this time that George and Harold realized that Mr. Krupp's face was no longer wet. It had been freeze-dried, along with everything else around them. So they snapped their fingers, and suddenly, our miraculous hero returned.

"Gee, it's a bit nippy today," said Captain Underpants.

"F-F-Forget about th-th-that n-n-n-now," said George, shivering. Quickly, he and Harold filled Captain Underpants in on the severity of the situation, and before long they all had a plan.

Captain Underpants flew out of Slightly
Younger Tiny Tippy's Robo-Glove and grabbed
his massive belt buckle. With one sensational
swoosh, Captain Underpants ripped Tippy's
pants, belt and all, right off of his Robo-Legs.

"HEY! No fair!!!" screamed Slightly Younger
Tiny Tippy, as he stood shivering in his gigantic
robotic boxer shorts.

Captain Underpants quickly tied the ripped pants legs in a knot and told everybody to climb aboard.

Soon, all of the good guys were tucked securely into the polyester/cotton blend trousers, and flying someplace safe and warm. They zipped across a vast ocean and finally came to a place that was not covered with ice. Captain Underpants swooped down and landed near the Chauvet-Pont-d'Arc Cave in Southern France.

George and Harold said good-bye to their cavepeople friends.

"We sure hope you like your new home here," said George.

"Keep drawing," said Harold. "And take care of our pals, Crackers and Sulu, OK?"

"Wait a minute," said George. "We can't leave our pets here. Crackers is sick! He needs to see a doctor!"

"Oh, yeah," said Harold, "I almost forgot! We've got to get to the future somehow."

Quickly, Captain Underpants flew George and Harold and Crackers and Sulu back to the frozen glaciers of North America. If they were ever going to get back to modern times, Slightly Younger Tiny Tippy was their best bet.

CHAPTER 19

THE VOW

When our five heroes finally reached Slightly Younger Tiny Tippy, he didn't seem at all surprised to see them.

"I'm not at all surprised to see you," said Slightly Younger Tiny Tippy, as he sipped casually from his water bottle. "I'll bet you guys want a ride back to the future, don't you?"

"We sure do!" said Captain Underpants. "Gee, that would be swell!"

Slightly Younger Tiny Tippy pointed his water bottle at Captain Underpants's face and squeezed.

SPLASH!

"W-What the heck is going on here?!!?" said
Mr. Krupp, as our five heroes began falling to
the frozen ground below.

"AAAAAAH!" screamed Harold. "WE'RE
DOOMED!"

Fortunately, Slightly Younger Tiny Tippy caught them before they hit the ground. But unfortunately, he had something even worse in mind for them than a 120-foot drop to their deaths.

As Slightly Younger Tiny Tippy set his Tinkle-Time Travelometer for a date in the upcoming future, George and Harold bemoaned their continually recurring predicament.

"Well, here we are again!" said George. "Back in the same mess we always end up in!"

"I know," said Harold. "It seems like every time we crack a joke or make a comic book, something terrible happens!"

"You know," said George, "if we ever get out of this mess, I think we should stop goofing around all the time."

"Yeah, I agree!" said Harold. "We need to quit making comic books and start paying more attention to our schoolwork!"

And as blue, crackling light began to envelop them, George and Harold made a vow to change their ways. They pledged to give up pranks and jokes and comic books, and they promised to begin taking life seriously and to start acting like responsible grown-ups.

"Wow!" said George, as they all disappeared into a crackling whirlpool of liquid time. "I feel more mature already!"

"Me, too!" said Harold.

CHAPTER 20
THIRTY YEARS FROM NOW

Suddenly, a giant ball of blue lightning exploded in the southern end of a busy midwestern city. George and Harold looked around them and saw the familiar sights of cars and houses and fast-food restaurants.

"We're HOME!" cried George.

"It sure seems that way," said Harold. "But how come everything looks so . . . *old*?!!?"

"Because we're not back where we started," laughed Slightly Younger Tiny Tippy. "We're thirty years in the future!"

IHOPe
THIS FOOD DOESN'T KILL ME!

"Why did we come to the *future*?" asked George.

"Because," said Tippy. "The last time I got rid of Captain Underpants, the whole world was destroyed. I just wanted to make sure that the world could survive the next thirty years without him, and it looks like it can!"

Tippy marched over to the elementary school and placed George and Harold and their two pets on the ground.

"Get comfortable, boys," said Tippy. "I'm about to DESTROY Captain Underpants once and for all, and I want you kids to have the best seats in the house!"

George and Harold looked up in horror as Slightly Younger Tiny Tippy began knocking Mr. Krupp around like a beanbag.

"I can't watch!" said Harold, as he petted his pet pterodactyl, who only seemed to be getting sicker.

Sulu scampered around the playground, finding twigs and branches and leaves, and weaving them into a nest to help keep Crackers warm.

"Remember," said George. "If we ever get out of this mess, we're going to straighten up and start acting like grown-ups!"

"That's right," said Harold, as he placed Crackers into the warm nest that Sulu had made. "We're going to be responsible and mature from now on!"

As Tippy kicked Mr. Krupp around like a soccer ball, George and Harold got distracted by a loud commotion behind them. Two teachers were yelling at the students on the playground, instructing them all to stop paying attention to the fierce struggle raging above them, and demanding that they straighten up and start acting like grown-ups.

As the battle intensified, the obnoxious teachers screamed louder and louder, hurling threats and insults at the curious students.

"Boy, I sure wish those two teachers would chill out," said George.

"I know," said Harold. "They're yelling so loud, I can't even hear the fight!"

Suddenly, a rusty green 2034 Honda Civic pulled into the parking lot, and a familiar-looking character came storming out. It was Mr. Krupp—only this was a thirty-year-*OLDER* version of Mr. Krupp. He was wrinklier than George and Harold were used to, with a scruffy white beard and mustache, and pants pulled up to his armpits.

Mr. Krupp marched toward the playground, opened up his mouth, and screamed four words that sent shivers down George's and Harold's spines.

"MR. BEARD! MR. HUTCHINS!"

George and Harold froze.

"Oh, NO!" whispered Harold. "Old Mr. Krupp recognized us!"

"What are we going to do?" asked George. "How are we EVER going to get out of *THIS MESS*???"

Old Mr. Krupp marched toward George and Harold, getting closer and closer as they shivered in horror. Then Old Man Krupp walked past George and Harold and continued walking toward the playground. "MR. BEARD! MR. HUTCHINS!" he screamed again. "GET THOSE KIDS INSIDE RIGHT NOW!!!"

"Who is he talking to?" asked George.

"I have no idea," said Harold.

Finally, the two screaming teachers turned around.

CHAPTER 21
GEORGE AND HAROLD'S
WORST NIGHTMARE

Do you know that feeling you get when your stomach sinks? It usually occurs just after the realization that something bad has happened or is going to happen. People often feel this way when they discover they forgot to study for a big test . . . or they're going to miss the school bus . . . or the giant gulp of milk they just swallowed expired three weeks ago.

Now imagine that feeling magnified about 1,000,000,000,000 times.

This is the feeling that occurred in George's and Harold's stomachs when the two obnoxious, screaming teachers turned around.

It was them.

More precisely, it was future versions of themselves. George and Harold had grown up to be teachers. But they weren't the nice, wonderful, imaginative teachers that *you* might be used to. No sir! George and Harold had evolved into the terrifying, boring, and vengeful teachers that *they* were used to.

Mr. Krupp squished between forty-year-old
Harold and thirty-nine-and-three-quarters-
year-old George, and slapped a sweaty arm
around each of them.

"I sure am glad you fellas are here," said
Mr. Krupp. "It's a tough job making everybody
miserable, isn't it?"

"It sure is, boss," said forty-year-old Harold.

"You know, it's hard to believe that you
guys used to be the craziest kids in this
school!" said Mr. Krupp. "Thank goodness you
both started taking life seriously!"

"Yeah," said thirty-nine-and-three-quarters-
year-old George. "One day about thirty years
ago, we saw the error of our ways. So we made
a vow to straighten up and fly right!"

"Yep!" said forty-year-old Harold. "From then on, it was nothing but serious study, strict discipline, and—and—*HEY, YOU KIDS, CUT THAT OUT!*"

George and Harold looked nervously at each other as their adult doubles continued screaming at the unfortunate children on the playground.

"Umm . . . remember that vow we just made to stop goofing around and start acting more like grown-ups?" asked Harold.

"Yeah," said George.

"I think we should vow a new vow that unvows the old vow we just vowed," said Harold.

"Let's get vowin'!" said George.

So as the terrifying battle raged above their heads, George and Harold shook hands and promised to always be themselves. They pledged to keep goofing around and to make even MORE comic books and to stop taking life so darned seriously.

"Let's daydream more, too!" said George.

"Yeah," said Harold. "Enough of this *sittin' still* and *payin' attention* stuff!"

As George and Harold vowed their new vows, something strange began to happen. A soft wind started to blow, the sound of wind chimes began to tinkle in the air, and the grown-up versions of George and Harold slowly disappeared. They vanished gradually at first. Then, after about a minute or so, Mr. Krupp was left standing there all by himself.

"Wow!" said George. "You mean it's that easy? All you have to do is make up your mind and stick to it, and you can change the future?"

"Yeah, I guess so," said Harold.

George and Harold walked up to Old Mr. Krupp, who was looking a little confused, and snapped their fingers. Suddenly, a familiar smile stretched across Old Mr. Krupp's face.

"Well?" said George, pointing up at the terrifying battle exploding above their heads. "What are you waiting for?"

"Yeah!" said Harold. "You're getting your butt kicked up there! Go help yourself!"

Quickly, Old Mr. Krupp tore off his clothes, dashed into the school, grabbed a red curtain from his office, and flew out of his window with a triumphant "Tra-La-Laaaaa!"

Old Captain Underpants immediately
rescued Mr. Krupp and brought him back
down to the ground.

"Wow! I'm sure glad that's over with!" said
Mr. Krupp.

"Relax, bub," said George. "You're just
getting started!"

And with a snap of George's and Harold's
fingers, Mr. Krupp returned to his heroic
self once again and flew into the sky to fight
alongside his future self.

CHAPTER 22
THE INCREDIBLY GRAPHIC VIOLENCE CHAPTER, PART 2 (IN FLIP-O-RAMA™)

FLIP-O-RAMA 4

(pages 187 and 189)

Remember, flip *only* page 187.
While you are flipping, be sure you
can see the picture on page 187
and the one on page 189.
If you flip quickly, the two
pictures will start to look like
<u>one</u> *animated* picture.

Don't forget to
add your own sound-effects!

LEFT HAND HERE

A FISTFUL OF
NOSE HAIRS

RIGHT
THUMB
HERE

RIGHT
INDEX
FINGER
HERE

188

A FISTFUL OF
NOSE HAIRS

FLIP-O-RAMA 5

(pages 191 and 193)

Remember, flip *only* page 191.
While you are flipping, be sure you
can see the picture on page 191
and the one on page 193.
If you flip quickly, the two
pictures will start to look like
<u>one</u> *animated* picture.

Don't forget to
add your own sound-effects!

LEFT HAND HERE

A SKY-HIGH
KICK IN THE EYE

RIGHT
THUMB
HERE

RIGHT
INDEX
FINGER
HERE

A SKY-HIGH
KICK IN THE EYE

FLIP-O-RAMA 6

(pages 195 and 197)

Remember, flip *only* page 195.
While you are flipping, be sure you
can see the picture on page 195
and the one on page 197.
If you flip quickly, the two
pictures will start to look like
<u>one</u> *animated* picture.

Don't forget to
add your own sound-effects!

LEFT HAND HERE

THE TOOTH HURTS

RIGHT
THUMB
HERE

196

THE TOOTH HURTS

CHAPTER 23
HOW THE UNIVERSE
REALLY BEGAN

Slightly Younger Tiny Tippy might have been ginormous and powerful, but he was no match for *TWO* Captain Underpantses. He fell to his massive robotic knees in a thunderous cloud of agonizing defeat.

BOOM

But Slightly Younger Tiny Tippy wasn't
ready to give up just yet.

He reached down to his control panel and
pressed the "Nuclear Bomb" button, which was
conveniently located between the "Strawberry
Milkshake" button and the Low-Fat Mint
Chocolate Chip Cookie dispenser. Suddenly, a
panel at the rear of the Robo-Boxers opened
up, and a 160-ton thermonuclear bomb
emerged.

"You might have defeated me," said Slightly
Younger Tiny Tippy, as he pressed the button
that started the countdown to doomsday, "but
I'll still get the last laugh!"

Suddenly, a light on the side of the bomb began to flash red. A computerized voice emanating from the bomb's arming system began the countdown:

"This bomb will detonate in sixty seconds," said the voice.

"NOOOO!" screamed George. "The last time one of those bombs went off, it killed all the dinosaurs!"

"But this bomb is WAY bigger than the last one," cried Harold. "This bomb could blow up the entire planet!"

"Correction," said Slightly Younger Tiny Tippy. "I've just activated my Graviton Levitator, which will give this bomb more destructive power than a *SUPERNOVA*! This thing's gonna blow up our entire GALAXY!"

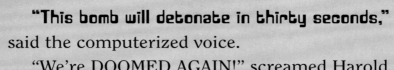

"This bomb will detonate in thirty seconds,"
said the computerized voice.

"We're DOOMED AGAIN!" screamed Harold.

"Well," said George. "It was fun while it
lasted! So long, old friend."

"Bye," said Harold.

As the two friends shook hands,
a huge gust of wind almost blew
them over.

It was
Crackers and
Sulu. George and
Harold's pets whooshed
by them as they flew up to
the opening of the radioactive
Robo-Boxers and fluttered down
to the command center inside. Sulu's
bionic brain quickly figured out the complex
control panel of the Tinkle-Time Travelometer,
and together the two animal friends began
mashing down the buttons on the switchboard.

"This bomb will detonate in fifteen seconds," said the computerized voice, as Crackers feverishly pecked at the controls. Finally, Sulu pushed down hard on the "Away We Go!" button, and the radioactive Robo-Boxers were enveloped in a gigantic ball of blue light.

Suddenly, the radioactive Robo-Boxers
(and their three occupants) were zapped back
in time 13.7 billion years ago. Back to a time
before time existed. Before ANYTHING existed.
There was no Earth, no sun, no planets, no
universe — there was nothing at all . . .

. . . except for the computerized countdown
on a 160-ton thermonuclear bomb:
    "This bomb will detonate in 5 . . . 4 . . .
3 . . . 2 . . . 1 . . ."

CHAPTER 24
TO MAKE A LONG
STORY SHORT

CHAPTER 25
THE BIG *KA-BLOOSH!* THEORY

The heat from the exploding supernova caused the universe to spring into existence and expand rapidly. As it expanded, it also began to cool, allowing its energy to be converted into lots of different subatomic particles.

It wasn't long before these particles combined to form atoms, which combined to form matter, which combined to form stars and planets and you and me and everything around us.

Scientists usually refer to this event as the "Big Bang Theory," but to be honest, the explosion sounded way more like a *Ka-Bloosh!* than a simple *bang*. I guess you just had to be there.

CHAPTER 26
WHAT HAVE WE LEARNED TODAY?

Remember at the beginning of this book when I told you you'd be smarter by page 210 than the world's most brilliant scientists? Well, congratulations. You now know what killed the dinosaurs, who started the last ice age, and how our universe actually began.

Unfortunately, this information is not something you can use for any practical benefits. So if you ever get tested on this stuff in school, please don't answer with the truth. I can guarantee you: It will NOT go well.

This is the unfortunate fate of super-smart people like us. There is rarely a place where we can use our vast knowledge, so we must be content to simply roll our eyes at people, shake our heads patronizingly, and sing that inspiring old song, "I'm Smarter Than You (Nyaa Nya Nya Nyaa Nyaaa)."

For your convenience, sheet music has been provided on the following page.

I'm Smarter Than You

Music and lyrics by Albert Einstine

I'm smarter than yoo - oou! Poo - py, poo - py, doo - doo!
I'm smarter than yoo - oou! Poo - py, poo - py, doo - doo!

You're dumber than mee - eee! Tin - kle, tin - kle, wee - wee!
You're dumber than mee - eee! Tin - kle, tin - kle, wee - wee!

Nyaa nya nya nyaa nyaaa, I know more than you.
Nyaa nya nya nyaa nyaaa, You know less than me.

Nyaa nya nya nyaa nyaaa, Tin - kle, tin - kle, doo - doo, doo - doo!
Nyaa nya nya nyaa nyaaa, Tin - kle, tin - kle, doo - doo, doo - doo!

(repeat ad nauseam)

CHAPTER 27
MEANWHILE, THIRTY
YEARS FROM NOW . . .

"Where did they go?" cried George, as he looked up into the sky where Tippy's radioactive Robo-Boxers had just stood.

"They disappeared!" said Harold. "They just vanished without a trace!"

Captain Underpants and his beardy old twin flew down to George and Harold. "What are we going to do now?" asked Old Captain Underpants.

"Why don't you go fly into that school and splash some water on your face," said Harold.

"Sure thing, boss!" said Old Captain Underpants. He flew straight to the nearest drinking fountain, and in no time at all, he returned to his crabby old, old self.

"Well," said George. "What *ARE* we going to do now? We're stuck in the future without a time machine!"

"Um . . . George?" said Harold, as he looked down at Crackers's nest.

"We've got no money . . . no identification . . . no *nothing*!" said George.

"Um . . . *George*?" said Harold again, looking closer into the nest.

"It's not like we can just go back to school and start over where we left off!" said George.

"Um . . . *George*?" said Harold a third time.

"*What?*" asked George finally.

Harold pointed at the nest that Sulu had made for Crackers. In the center of the nest were three purple-and-orange-speckled eggs.

George's mouth dropped open. "WHAT ARE *THOSE*?" he cried.

"I guess Crackers wasn't sick after all!" said Harold. "He was *pregnant*!"

"But Crackers is a BOY! Boys can't lay eggs!"

"Maybe Crackers is a girl," said Harold.

"Oh, yeah," said George. "I guess that would make more sense."

George and Harold carefully picked up the eggs and examined them. "We've got to keep these eggs warm until Crackers and Sulu get back," said George.

"But we don't know where they went!" said Harold. "We don't even know if they WILL be back!"

"Then we're just going to have to raise these eggs on our own," said George. "That's the least we can do!"

CHAPTER 28
THE FINAL CHAPTER
OF THE VERY LAST
CAPTAIN UNDERPANTS
EPIC NOVEL

George and Harold and Captain Underpants
each held an egg close to their bodies to keep
them warm. Then they started walking.

"Where are we going to go?" asked Harold.

"I guess we should try our houses first,"
said George. "Maybe our parents still live there."

"Good idea," said Harold.

Suddenly, a bright ball of flashing light appeared in front of them. The flashing got more and more intense, until it finally exploded with a blast of crackling lightning.

And there, where the flashing ball of light had been, was a gigantic, glow-in-the-dark robotic squid. The top of the Robo-Squid opened, and George and Harold's nemesis, Melvin Sneedly, popped his head up.

"Greetings," said Melvin. "I have come from the past to bring you guys back home!"

"Hey, wait a minute!" said George incredulously. "How did you know where to find us?"

"Let's just say an *old friend* led me to you," said Melvin.

"OK," said George.

"Works for me," said Harold.

"You see," Melvin continued, "when I designed Sulu's robotic endoskeleton, I installed a—"

"BO-*RING*!" said George, interrupting.

"Yeah," said Harold. "We stopped listening, like, ten seconds ago."

"WELL, LISTEN TO THIS!" Melvin shouted, as he reached down and grabbed our heroes with his Robo-Squid arms. "You three losers—and your precious eggs—are coming with me!"

"Where are you taking us?" cried George.

"You'll see soon enough," Melvin laughed maniacally. "You'll see soon enough!"

Suddenly, the gigantic, glow-in-the-dark, time-traveling Supa Squid began to shake and sputter in a buzzing ball of electrified light.

"Oh, NO!" cried George.

"Here we go again!" cried Harold.

ABOUT THE
AUTHOR-ILLUSTRATOR

When Dav Pilkey was a kid, he was diagnosed with ADHD and dyslexia. Dav was so disruptive in class that his teachers made him sit out in the hallway every day. Luckily, Dav loved to draw and make up stories. He spent his time in the hallway creating his own original comic books — the very first adventures of Dog Man and Captain Underpants.

In college, Dav met a teacher who encouraged him to illustrate and write. He won a national competition in 1986 and the prize was the publication of his first book, WORLD WAR WON. He made many other books before being awarded the 1998 California Young Reader Medal for DOG BREATH, which was published in 1994, and in 1997 he won the Caldecott Honor for THE PAPERBOY.

THE ADVENTURES OF SUPER DIAPER BABY, published in 2002, was the first complete graphic novel spin-off from the Captain Underpants series and appeared at #6 on the USA Today bestseller list for all books, both adult and children's, and was also a New York Times bestseller. It was followed by THE ADVENTURES OF OOK AND GLUK: KUNG FU CAVEMEN FROM THE FUTURE and SUPER DIAPER BABY 2: THE INVASION OF THE POTTY SNATCHERS, both USA Today bestsellers. The unconventional style of these graphic novels is intended to encourage uninhibited creativity in kids.

His stories are semi-autobiographical and explore universal themes that celebrate friendship, tolerance, and the triumph of the good-hearted.

Dav loves to kayak in the Pacific Northwest with his wife.